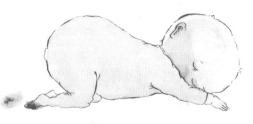

Gracie's Baby Chub Chop

G i l l i a n   J o h n s o n

Tundra Books

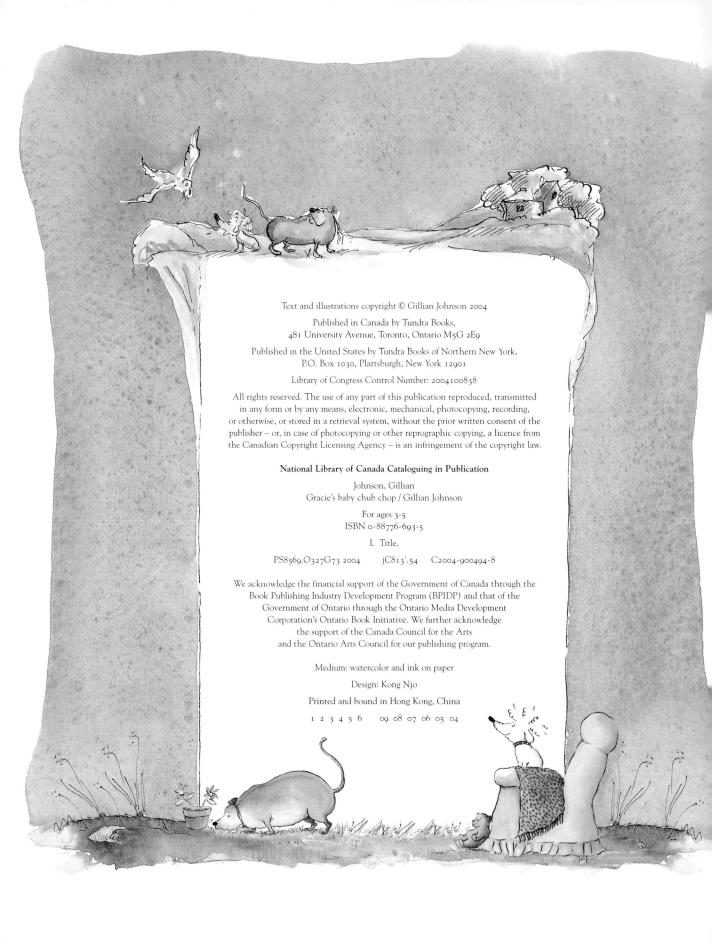

Text and illustrations copyright © Gillian Johnson 2004

Published in Canada by Tundra Books,
481 University Avenue, Toronto, Ontario M5G 2E9

Published in the United States by Tundra Books of Northern New York,
P.O. Box 1030, Plattsburgh, New York 12901

Library of Congress Control Number: 2004100838

National Library of Canada Cataloguing in Publication

Johnson, Gillian
Gracie's baby chub chop / Gillian Johnson

For ages 3-5
ISBN 0-88776-693-5

I. Title.

PS8569.O327G73 2004   jC813'.54   C2004-900494-8

We acknowledge the financial support of the Government of Canada through the
Book Publishing Industry Development Program (BPIDP) and that of the
Government of Ontario through the Ontario Media Development
Corporation's Ontario Book Initiative. We further acknowledge
the support of the Canada Council for the Arts
and the Ontario Arts Council for our publishing program.

Medium: watercolor and ink on paper

Design: Kong Njo

Printed and bound in Hong Kong, China

1 2 3 4 5 6   09 08 07 06 05 04

For Karen and Joseph

and little Chub Chop

Gracie and Fabio had it all –
Two bones to chew, a rubber ball,
A teddy bear, an apple tree,
A furry rug, a family.

A perfect life in every way –

Then Baby Chub Chop came to stay.

"We've won a trip to Timbuktu!
Our treasure will be safe with you."

But Baby Chub was full of flaws,
He had no tail, no fur, no paws.
He lay about
On back and tummy,
Sucking on
A rubber dummy.

His head was bald.
He had a rash.
He ate the most disgusting mash.

Nevertheless,
The family fussed,
Coogled, gurgled,
SHUSHED! and HUSHED!
"A little angel," Father said,
As Mother put Chub Chop to bed.

The presence of this clumsy lump,
Who couldn't walk or run or jump,
Was not so bad for Gracie, who
Could tolerate a week or two.

Her brother, on the other hand,
Decided that he could not stand
The dada-gaga way it spoke,
The waa-waa-waaing when it woke.
(But more than that, he was afraid
That all his things would be mislaid.)

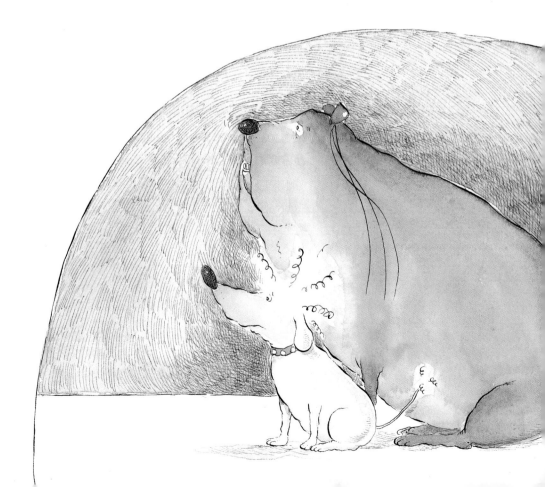

It happened on the second morning.
Fabio gave the Chub a warning:

"Stay away.
Leave me alone.
Don't touch my rug,
My ball, my bone."

Chub Chop grinned,
He drooled and chewed,
He hiccupped up a bit of food.
"You are no angel, that I know,"
To Baby Chub said Fabio.

But Gracie wasn't
Really sure
What angels weren't
Or angels were.

Until the day they were at home –
Father and baby on their own –
Chub Chop found that he was able

To stand up tall beside the table!

And burbling a little Chub-Chop tune,
He reached for a lovely red balloon.
He held the string,
He stepped, he toddled,
He flashed a toothless grin,
Then waddled.

One step, two,

He tripped, he sprawled,

He stood back up, he fell, he crawled.

And moving thus, he lurched his way

To where the doggies liked to play.

(Gracie and Fabio

Had gone to the park

To sniff the world till it was dark.

Or else they might have put a stop

To pillaging, plundering Baby Chop.)

So, off went Chub
With ball and bone,
And hey, why not?

The telephone!

The brushes, the leashes, Mother's flippers,
Fabio's kibbles and Gracie's kippers.
The teddy, the pillow, and Fabio's rug,
A china plate, a christening mug.

The children's puzzles, a truck, a fairy,
A hairy monster known as Larry.
Baby Chub Chop's cheeks were pink.

Oops! There went Mother's pot of ink!
Such lovely patterns on the floor –
He gurgled as he made some more.

Throughout the baby's busy caper,
Father sat and read the paper.

When he looked up, the tot was asleep.
He put him down without a peep.

He didn't notice all the mess.
(Some people don't, I must confess.)

But Gracie and Fabio
Knew when they came
Home from the park
That Chub was to blame.

The house was a muddle,
He'd scattered their stuff.
"That *angel's* in trouble!
Enough is enough!"

But Mother blamed *them*
When she came home that night.
She didn't ask questions.
She wasn't polite!
"To the doghouse!" she said,
Then she started to shout.
She locked them outside.
She sent them without

Their kibbles and kippers,
Their ball and their bone.
"Everything's missing!
Now where is that phone?"

Out in the doghouse
Fabio was moping
While Gracie was sniffing,
Searching, hoping,
To find the scent to lead her to
The things they'd lost.
And then –

A clue!

Over by the flower bed
She sniffed and snuffed,
She trod, she tread.

Till underneath the hollyhocks
She came across the puzzle box!!

Through a window
Gracie squeezed.
She huffed and puffed,
She strained and wheezed.
"Now what is this?"
She asked, quite pleased.
The teddy, the pillow, and Fabio's rug,
A china plate, a christening mug!

The kibbles and kippers
She found in the tub,
Then chasing the trail
Of the inky-toed Chub
She spied Mother's flippers,
In an old crystal jug.

Out in the laundry room
Gracie uncovered
The phone in the dryer

And then she discovered
The bone and the ball
In the washing machine.
Out they came – wet –
But at least they were clean!

She piled the loot,
And galumphed out of sight,
Wagging her tail
With enormous delight.

Then the doorbell rang,
The baby cried.
Mother shrieked.
Father sighed.

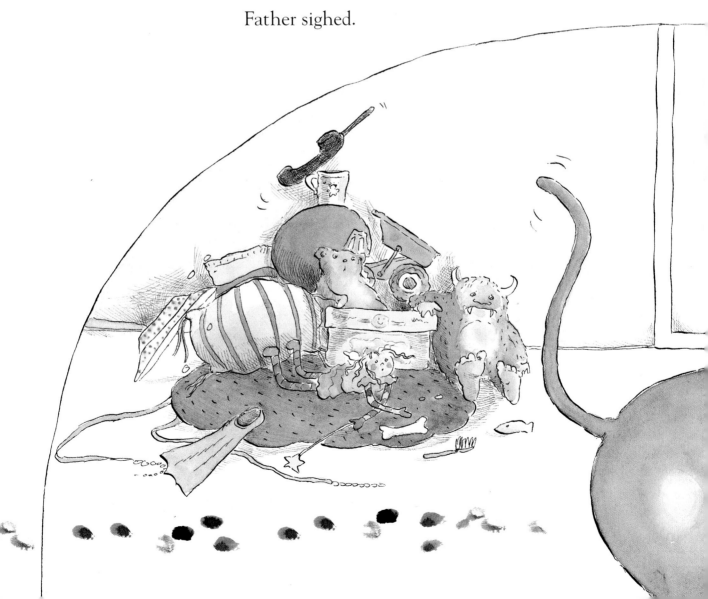

"Baby Chub!"

His parents called.

They kissed his little head so bald.

They wiped his tears, they tweaked his nose,

And suddenly, in horror, froze.

They looked and saw the awful mess.
(Some people do, I must confess.)
And so that no one else could hear,
One whispered in the other's ear,
"No wonder our treasure's such a grump.
This house is a disgusting dump."
They scooped up Chub,
And bid adieu.
"A shame we didn't take you, too.
It was *so* much cleaner in Timbuktu."

Now Gracie and Fabio knew what to do.
They escorted their family to the clue.

An inky footprint in full view.
First one. Then another. Another two.
Footprints belonging to –

You-Know-Who!

"Oh no! Poor dogs!
We got it wrong.
It was the *baby*
All along!"

Mother kissed Gracie
Then Fabio.

She hugged them both.
"Well, now we know,
When little angels
Start to walk,
They must be watched
Around the clock!"